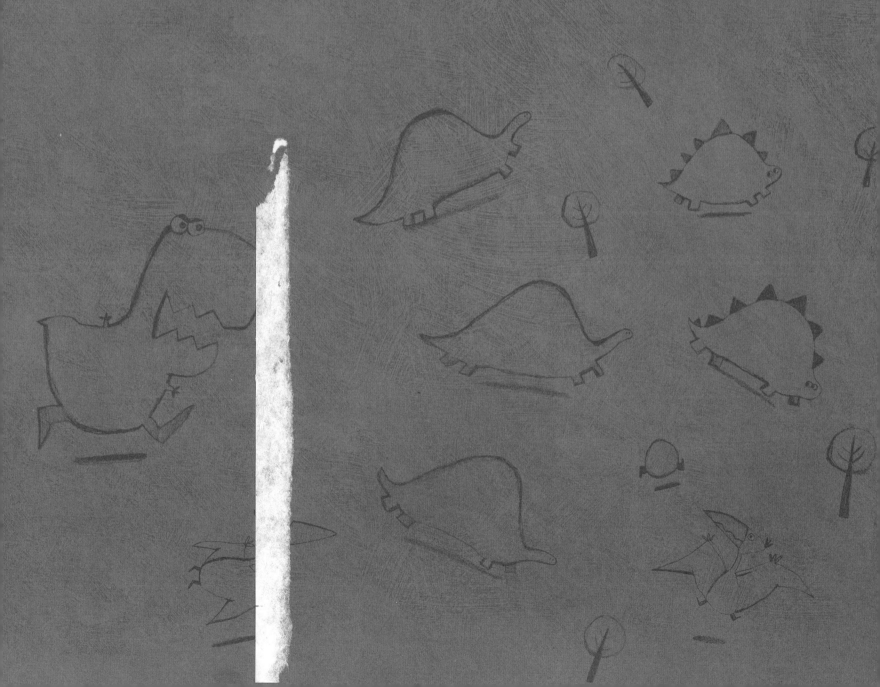

To Daisy May - M.K

For Ava, Paul and Ali - M.McQ

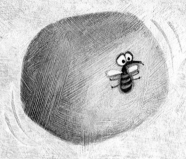

Baby Blue Egg
First published in 2008
by Hodder Children's Books

Text copyright © Mij Kelly 2008
Illustrations copyright © Mary McQuillan 2008

Hodder Children's Books
338 Euston Road
London NW1 3BH

Hodder Children's Books Australia
Level 17/207 Kent Street
Sydney NSW 2000

A catalogue record of this book is available from the British Library.

HB ISBN: 978 0 340 95690 8
PB ISBN: 978 0 340 95691 5
10 9 8 7 6 5 4 3 2 1

Printed in China

Hodder Children's Books is a division of Hachette Children's Books
An Hachette Livre UK Company

www.hachettelivre.co.uk

Mij Kelly

BABY BLUE EGG

Mary McQuillan

A division of Hachette Children's Books

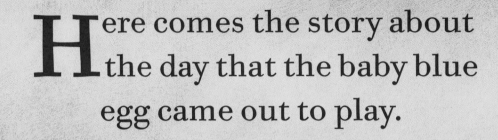

Here comes the story about the day that the baby blue egg came out to play.

First
came
one
leg...

then
came
the
other...

High in a ginko
tree something
red twittered
and flittered
and shook with
dread, and pointed
with one trembling
wing...

'Oh please don't wake
the scary thing!'

Too late. Too late.
She was already awake
and the snarl on her face would
make your heart quake,
and the size of her teeth
would make your knees shake,
and to stand there and wait
would be a mistake...

'Run for cover!
Run for cover!
Run, little egg,
and find your
mother!'

The baby blue egg ran.
He ran as fast as little
legs can.

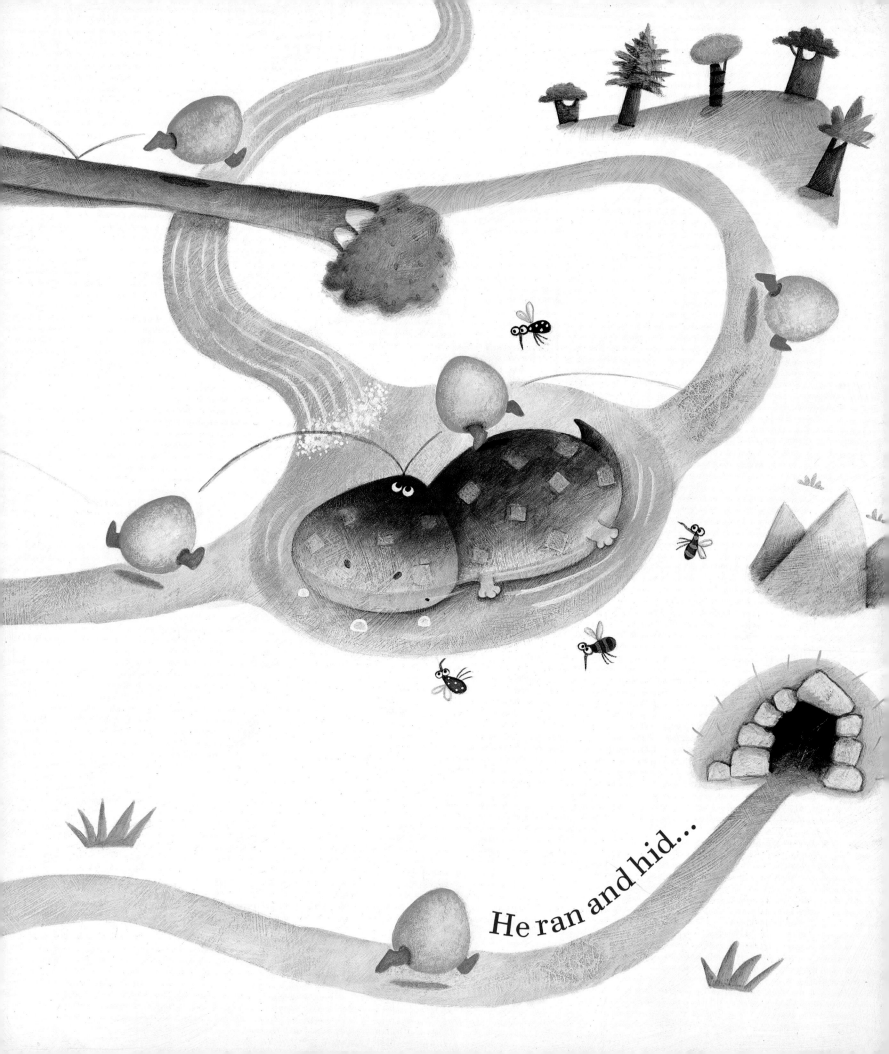

He ran and hid…

under
**something
yellow –**
an exceedingly spiky,
spiny fellow.

'Too late! Too late!
She's already awake!
Run for your lives,
for goodness sake!'

And all around was a terrible
sound, the sound of trees ripped
out of the ground, ripped out
of the ground and thrown
all around…

'Run for cover!
Run for cover!
Run, little egg,
and find your mother!'

The yellow thing ran.
He ran just as fast
as a baby egg can.

He ran and hid...

under
something green.

'An egg with legs?
What can this mean?'

'Are you my mother?'
said the baby blue egg.

'No, little egg,'
the green thing said.
'And please do
stop this hullabaloo,
or you might wake up
you-know-who...'

'Too late! Too late!
She's already awake!
Run for your lives,
for goodness sake!'

And all around was a terrible
sound, the sound of rocks torn
out of the ground, torn out
of the ground and thrown
all around...

'Run for cover!
Run for cover!
Run, little egg, and find
your mother!'

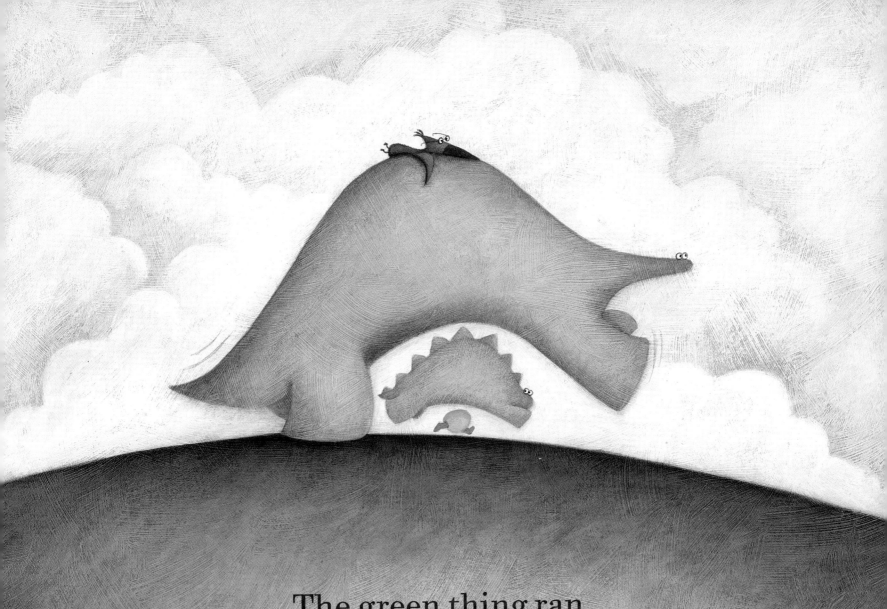

The green thing ran.
He ran just as fast as a yellow
thing can.

And also as fast as a baby blue egg
(which can run very fast
on its baby blue legs).

He ran slap bang into...

something
blue.

'Hello, Scary Thing! How do you do?'

Well the scary thing was most polite.
She didn't bite. She didn't fight.
She didn't roar or show her claws.
She kept her teeth inside her jaws – and
burst into floods of tears instead!

'To tell the truth,
I'm sad,' she said.
'I'm sad because...

'**Hey**,
does this egg
belong to you?'

'Run for cover!
Run for cover!
One scary thing
was bad enough…